The Colossal Catfish

Becky Freeman
Illustrated by
Matt Archambault

A Faith Parenting Guide can be found on page 32.

Faith Kids™ is an imprint of
Cook Communications Ministries, Colorado Springs, Colorado 80918
Cook Communications, Paris, Ontario
Kingsway Communications, Eastbourne, England

THE COLOSSAL CATFISH
© 2000 by Becky Freeman for text and Matthew Archambault for illustrations.

Faith Kids™ is a registered trademark of Cook Communications Ministries.

Published in association with the literary agency of Alive Communications, Inc., 1465 Kelly
Johnson Blvd., Suite 320, Colorado Springs, CO 80920.

Edited by Jeannie Harmon
Designed by Ya Ye Design

Scripture taken from the *Holy Bible: New International Version®.* copyright © 1973, 1978, 1984 by
International Bible Society. Used by permission of Zondervan Publishing House. All rights
reserved.

First printing, 2000
Printed in Singapore
04 03 02 01 00   5 4 3 2 1

Library of Congress Cataloging-in-Publication Data

Freeman, Becky, 1959-
     The colossal catfish/Becky Freeman: illustrated by Matt Archambault.
        p.   cm. — (Gabe & critters)
     Summary: Gabe has been longing for a pet fish and believes God had answered his prayer
in a special way when a colossal catfish nudges him as he fishes in a nearby pond. Includes
questions and answers about catfish.
     ISBN 0-7814-3340-1
     [1. Catfishes Fiction. 2. Fishes Fiction. 3. Christian life Fiction.] I. Archambault,
Matthew, ill.   II. Title.   III. Series: Freeman, Becky, 1959-   Gabe & critters.
PZ7.F874635Co   2000
[E]—-dc21
                                                                                        99-41925
                                                                                               CIP

Dedicated to:
My youngest son, Gabe,
a true critter-lover and
the inspiration for this series.
Thanks for the "worm" memories
. . . and for the hugs.
Love,
Mom

"Please, please, pleeeeeease," Gabe begged his brothers, using his whiniest voice. "Please stop at the pet store!"

Zeke glanced over at Zach who was driving the truck. "What do you think? Should we let these guys loose in a pet store? What if the owner thinks they're monkeys and they get locked up in a cage or something?"

Zach grinned and winked. "Yeah, I don't know. . . ."

"Pleeeeeeeeeeeease!" The voices of two boys rang out from the back seat.

"Okay," said Zach as he steered the car into the shopping center parking lot, "but we can only stay a few minutes. Mom said to be back home by two and I want to stop for burgers and fries before then. Deal?"

"Deal!" shouted Gabe as he hurried Josh out of the truck and into O'Malley's Pet Store.

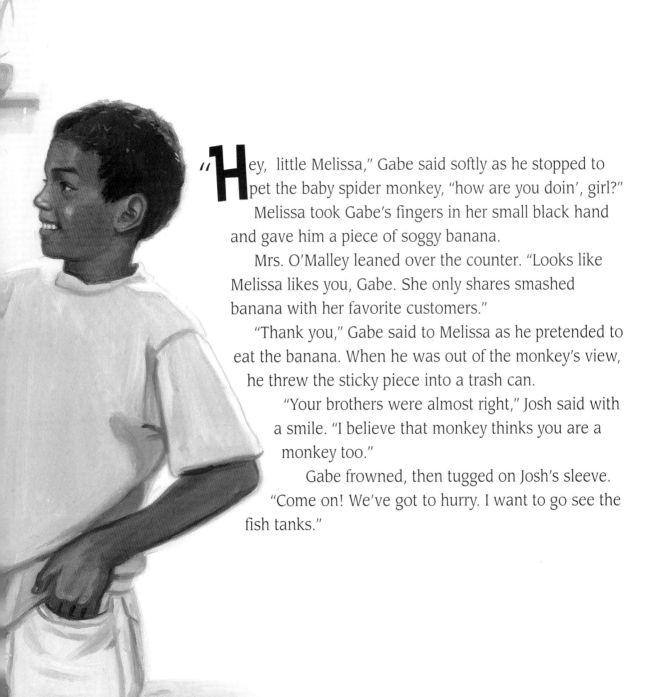

"Hey, little Melissa," Gabe said softly as he stopped to pet the baby spider monkey, "how are you doin', girl?"

Melissa took Gabe's fingers in her small black hand and gave him a piece of soggy banana.

Mrs. O'Malley leaned over the counter. "Looks like Melissa likes you, Gabe. She only shares smashed banana with her favorite customers."

"Thank you," Gabe said to Melissa as he pretended to eat the banana. When he was out of the monkey's view, he threw the sticky piece into a trash can.

"Your brothers were almost right," Josh said with a smile. "I believe that monkey thinks you are a monkey too."

Gabe frowned, then tugged on Josh's sleeve. "Come on! We've got to hurry. I want to go see the fish tanks."

7

There was something amazing about the aquarium room. Gabe loved listening to the gurgling sounds of the fish tanks. He loved watching the brightly colored tropical fish swim, float, and dive gently through the water. This room full of fish always made Gabe feel happy and a little sleepy at the same time.

"Man, oh man," Gabe said, his nose pressed against the aquarium's glass. "I'd love to have pet fish and an aquarium."

"Yeah," said Josh as he watched a clown fish dart in and out of a sea anemone. "But look at the prices on these tanks. It would cost about a whole year's allowance to buy all this fancy fish stuff."

Just then, Zach called out, "Gabe! Josh! Time to go!"

The boys waved a sad good-bye to the fish. As they walked by Melissa's cage on the way out the door, the baby monkey reached through the bars, grabbed a piece of Gabe's shirt, and smashed her last piece of banana into it.

"Why Melissa O'Malley," Mrs. O'Malley scolded the monkey, "you leave that poor boy alone! He is NOT a monkey!"

Zach, Zeke, and Joshua laughed about Gabe's monkey friend all the way home. Gabe didn't think it was all THAT funny.

That evening, Gabe walked out on the porch and plopped down on the porch swing.

"Dear God," he prayed as he gazed at the stars, "You made some wonderful critters in this world. Even if some of them, like spider monkeys, are a little messy. I can't believe You thought up so many fish in so many different colors. You are an awesome God!"

After school the next day, Josh came home with Gabe.

"I'm hungry!" Josh exclaimed as he set his backpack on the kitchen table.

"Me, too," agreed Gabe. "Let's have a snack!"

Mom was busy in the garden watering her roses, so Josh and Gabe went into the kitchen, pulled a couple of corn dogs out of the freezer, zapped them in the microwave and wandered out to the dock. Once there, they took off their shoes and dangled their feet in the water as they munched on their snack-on-a-stick.

"Whatcha thinkin' about?" asked Josh, noticing Gabe seemed quiet today.

Gabe swallowed a bite of his corn dog and answered, "I was just wishing I could have a pet fish of my own." As Gabe talked, bits of cornmeal fell off the corn dog and into the pond.

Suddenly, Gabe felt something tickle his toe.

"Quit it!" he yelled.

"Quit what?" Josh asked in surprise.

"Quit touching my toe with your foot."

"I'm not touching your toe, Gabe. Look! I'm too far away."

"Then what was that?"

"I don't . . .WHOA!" Josh pointed at the water's surface.

"Whoa what?" asked Gabe.

"Whoa, look by your toe."

Gabe looked down and nearly fell into the pond. By Gabe's feet, nibbling at corn dog pieces and his toes, was the biggest catfish Gabe had ever seen. It was bigger than a turtle. It was bigger than his little dog, Colonel. Gabe stood up to get a better look.

"Oh, WOW! That catfish is huge—it's gigantic!"

"It's colossal!" finished Josh. "Yes, Colossal the Catfish—that's what we'll call him."

"Hey," said Josh, "I wonder if he could be your pet fish?"

"I wonder . . ." said Gabe as he watched the huge fish sink below the water and head toward a place under the dock.

The next afternoon after school, Gabe ran straight to the pond. He carried a tub full of catfish treats with him. Zach and Zeke had given him their secret recipe for catfish cookies.

"They love this stuff," Zach told him.

"Yeah," said Zeke, "Zach and I caught about fifteen catfish last night with this bait."

"But I don't want to catch the fish," said Gabe. "I just want to feed him and be his friend."

23

Sure enough, as soon as Gabe's catfish treats hit the water, VRRRRUMPH! up jumped Colossal, eager for more. This happened every day until one day, before Gabe even threw the food into the water, Colossal heard him coming and jumped out of the water in excitement.

The next day, Gabe found Josh on the playground at recess and told him about what Colossal had done.

"I didn't get an aquarium," said Gabe, "but I got something even better—a whole pond, with the biggest, jumpiest pet fish in the county! And the best part is I don't have to change the water or clean out the tank! God thinks of everything. He even knows how to give me better things that I ask for sometimes."

"Like what?" asked Josh.

"Well, last year I prayed for a video game, but I never got it. Instead, God gave me something a whole lot better. He gave me someone to talk to and play with every day, someone to be my best friend. God gave me you, Josh."

Josh grinned and thought for a minute. "Gabe, if I were a baby monkey, I'd give you a piece of smashed banana."

The two friends laughed out loud.

Just then, the school bell rang. Gabe and Josh raced toward their classroom, thinking happy thoughts about silly monkeys, giant fish, and long recesses. But their happiest thoughts were about God's special gift to them—the gift of a colossal friendship.

Gabe's Fun Catfish Facts

1. How did catfish get their name?
Catfish got their name because whiskery "barbels" come out of the corners of their mouths. These whiskers look a lot like the whiskers of the cat. Actually, catfish use their "whiskers" to help them feel around for food.

2. What do catfish eat when they can't get corn dogs?
Catfish will eat just about anything that's lying around on the bottom of the lake or pond. They especially like minnows, crayfish, worms, chicken livers, and bread balls. They love dough baits that have a strong smell, such as cheese or garlic. Many fishermen use "stink bait" that they buy at the bait stores to attract the fish. If you've ever smelled a jar of that stuff, you'll know why they call it "stink bait."

3. When do catfish usually come out?
Catfish like to come out and look for food at night.

4. What is the biggest catfish ever caught in America?
In July, 1996, a man caught a blue catfish out of the Tennessee River that weighed 111 pounds. This is the biggest catfish caught in America on record.

5. What's the biggest catfish in the world?
The biggest catfish is found in Eastern Europe. It is called a *wel* and it comes out at night to eat large fish, frogs, and even ducks. It can grow to be ten feet long and can weigh 440 pounds!

6. How do catfish lay eggs?

The father catfish sweeps an area on the bottom of the pond clean with his body. When the bottom of the "nest" is clean and firm, the mother fish lays about 10,000 eggs. After the eggs are laid, the father fish takes over the care of the babies.

First, he "shoos" the mother away. Then, using his fins, he fans the eggs to make sure they get plenty of air bubbles. Then he guards the nest, scaring off any intruders, until the young fish hatch and become about an inch long.

7. What are some strange kinds of catfish?

The upside down catfish from Africa actually swims upside down. This way it can eat the green algae that grows on the underside of water plant leaves.

There is also a walking catfish. This powerful fish can breathe air as it actually walks across marshy areas in Florida searching for food. What would you think if you ran into a FISH while you were taking a walk?

8. Where do catfish like to hide?

Freshwater catfish like to hide in hollow logs, under banks, and in underwater brush. If these are removed from a lake or pond, there won't be as many catfish the next year.

9. Aren't all catfish kind of gray and ugly?

Actually, in South America, catfish come in beautiful colors. The red-tailed catfish, from the Amazon River has a beautiful yellow strip down it's sides and a bright red tail.

Colossal Catfish Cookie

Roll out one refrigerated package of sugar cookie dough. Divide dough in half.

Roll and pat one half of the dough into an oblong shape, the other into a triangle. Overlap the circle a bit over the triangle "tail," press to make into the shape of a fish.

Bake at 350 on a flat cookie sheet for 15-20 minutes, until golden brown.

Then frost and decorate with canned milk chocolate frosting, using thin strips of licorice to make catfish "whiskers", and an "M & M" candy for an eye. Cover body with slivered almonds to make fishy scales.

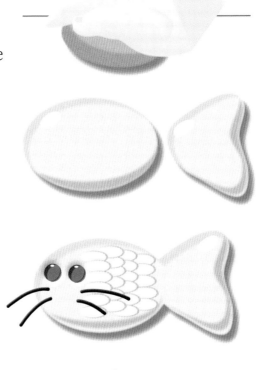

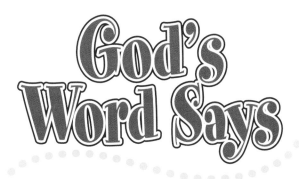

God's Word Says

A friend loves at all times.

Proverbs 17:17 (NIV)

Faith Parenting Guide

The Colossal Catfish

Age: 4-7 years old

Life Issue: My child needs to understand that having good friends is important.

Spiritual Building Block: Friendship

Learning Styles

Sight: Watch a video that addresses friendship. *Homeward Bound, Little Rascals,* a number of the Disney videos, etc. are examples. Talk to your child about what qualities a friend has and how he or she could be a better friend to others.

Sound: Retell the story of David and Jonathan's friendship from 1 Samuel 18:1-16, 19-20. How do we know that David and Jonathan were friends? What did Jonathan do for David to show his friendship? How do we show our friends that they are important to us?

Touch: Put a small item in each of ten numbered bags. Have family members open each bag and without peeking, feel the item inside. Instruct them to write down what item is in each bag (children that cannot write will need assistance). When finished, compare notes. By looking at the sack, was there any way to tell what was inside? Can you know if a person will be a friend until you know what is in his or her heart?

Excerpted from p. 97 of *An Introduction to Family Nights* by Jim Weidmann and Kurt Bruner, ©1997, Chariot Victor Publishing.